Godfather Drosselmeyer

Marie

Sugarplum Fairy

The Nutcracker

Fritz

The Mouse King

This Ladybird Book

belongs to

....

LADYBIRD BOOKS

UK | USA | Canada | Ireland | Australia | India | New Zealand | South Africa

Ladybird Books is part of the Penguin Random House group of companies
whose addresses can be found at global.penguinrandomhouse.com.

www.penguin.co.uk   www.puffin.co.uk   www.ladybird.co.uk

Penguin
Random House
UK

First published 2020

001

Adapted from E. T. A. Hoffman's original story by Rhiannon Findlay

Illustrated by Romina Galotta

Copyright © Ladybird Books Ltd, 2020

Printed in China

A CIP catalogue record for this book is available from the British Library

ISBN: 978–0–241–41624–2

All correspondence to:
Ladybird Books, Penguin Random House Children's
One Embassy Gardens, 8 Viaduct Gardens, London SW11 7BW

THE NUTCRACKER

This story is adapted from the original tale by E. T. A. Hoffman, from which many ballet productions of *The Nutcracker* take their inspiration.

Adapted by
Rhiannon Findlay

Illustrated by
Romina Galotta

It was Christmas Eve,
and the snow outside was
beginning to fall. In the house
at the end of the street, Marie
and her brother, Fritz, were
getting ready for a party.

The room had been decorated, and in the corner
stood a wonderful Christmas tree, covered in
twinkling lights, tiny sugared almonds and,
at the very top, a beautiful pink sugarplum fairy.

As the party guests began to arrive, Marie spotted her godfather through the crowd. Godfather Drosselmeyer was a famous toymaker – and he always arrived with gifts for Fritz and Marie!

Once the party had started, Godfather Drosselmeyer called the children over so he could reveal their presents.

Sat on the table was a splendid castle, with
golden towers and rooms, filled with miniature people.
The castle was being protected by model horses and
an army of toy soldiers in bright red uniforms.

While her brother began to play with the toy soldiers,
Marie spotted a large, curious wooden man
on the edge of the table.

He was also wearing
a smart uniform,
long black boots and
a fine-looking hat.
But the thing that struck
Marie most was his face,
for the man was
smiling up at her.

"Aha," said Godfather Drosselmeyer.
"I see you have
found the Nutcracker."

Godfather Drosselmeyer explained
that he had made the Nutcracker
especially for Marie. He told her
that it was a very special toy,
with many magical secrets.

Suddenly Fritz, who was no longer interested
in playing with the smaller toy soldiers,
pulled the Nutcracker out of
his sister's hands, and –

snap!

The Nutcracker's jaw
broke in two.

"You must look after your Nutcracker," said Godfather Drosselmeyer as he mended the toy. "He may look like a strong soldier, but you are his protector, Marie."

Later that night, Marie
couldn't sleep. She crept
downstairs and tiptoed
over to the Christmas tree.

She picked up the Nutcracker. Then, at long last,
she lay down under the tree and fell asleep.

Marie awoke to the sound of the clock striking **midnight**.

She looked up at the Christmas tree.

It seemed to be growing **taller** . . .

and taller . . . .

Or was *she* getting smaller and smaller?

Hearing a noise, Marie turned around and was astonished to see her
Nutcracker walking towards her – followed by his army of toy soldiers!
Before she could make sense of it, there came a scuttling sound,
and into the room poured hundreds of mice. Then, from out of the
shadows, came the most enormous mouse Marie had ever seen.

"The Mouse King!" gasped the Nutcracker.

"ATTACK!" cried the Mouse King.

"TO BATTLE!"
called the brave Nutcracker.

With a cheer, the toy soldiers
raised their swords and ran towards
the army of mice, who were
squeaking and gnashing
their sharp little teeth.

During the battle,
the Nutcracker became so busy that
he did not see the Mouse King
sneaking up behind him.

From across the room,
Marie saw her Nutcracker
in trouble and thought quickly.

She pulled off one
of her slippers and

threw it

at the Mouse King.

The enormous mouse fell to the ground,
and the crown tumbled from his head.

THUD!

The battle had been won.

As the mice scurried away, the Nutcracker picked up the
golden crown and gave it to Marie. "Thank you," he said.
"You saved my life. Let me take you somewhere truly magical."

Holding her hand, the Nutcracker led Marie through
a small secret door that had appeared in the wall.

On the other side of the door was the most beautiful forest Marie had ever seen! The trees glittered and sparkled like diamonds, and each one had silver fruits and sugared almonds hanging from its branches.

"Welcome to the Land of Sweets," said the Nutcracker.

The pair soon arrived at a rippling lake. The water was the softest pink, and the smell of roses filled the air.

A curious little boat lay bobbing on the water, as though it had been waiting for them.

Stepping in, Marie and the Nutcracker began to magically glide across the Lake of Roses.

On the other side of the lake stood a magnificent castle –
that appeared to be made entirely of sweets!
"Look," said the Nutcracker. "That's Marzipan Castle.
It's where the Sugarplum Fairy lives."

A fairy in a sparkling
pink-and-white dress greeted them.
"Welcome," said the Sugarplum Fairy.
"You have arrived just in time –
the dancing is about to begin."

The sound of music filled the air,
and Marie and the Nutcracker watched
as performers from faraway lands
took it in turns to dance.

They leapt and fluttered
across the room in wonderful
explosions of colour.

But **nothing** compared to the dance
of the **Sugarplum Fairy**.

She twirled quickly and gracefully, spinning
faster and faster, until the room became a blur,
and Marie's tired eyes began to close . . .

When Marie woke up on Christmas morning,
she was surprised to find herself lying
under the Christmas tree.

"You won't believe the adventures I've had!"
she said to her mother, and she told her
all about the Nutcracker and the Mouse King
and the dance of the Sugarplum Fairy.

"It sounds like a wonderful dream," said her mother, "but it was only a dream, Marie. See the wooden Nutcracker in your arms and the fairy on top of the tree?"

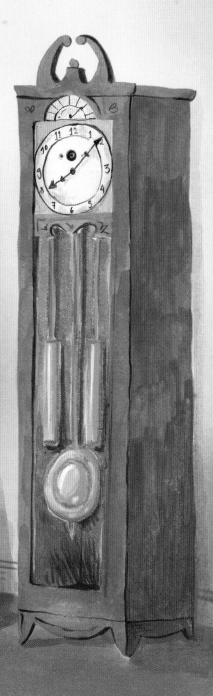

For a moment, Marie was quiet.

Then she reached into her pocket and found a tiny golden crown.
With a smile, she placed it on the Nutcracker's head
and whispered, "I'll see you next Christmas Eve."